# The Lost Umbrellas of Lexington

Written by Meredith Newman

Illustrated by Carly Beck

ethos
collective

Published by Ethos CollectiveTM,
PO Box 43
Powell, OH 43065
EthosCollective.VIP

LCCN: 2022919358
Paperback ISBN: 978-1-63680-107-0
Hardback ISBN: 978-1-63680-108-7
e-Book ISBN: 978-1-63680-109-4

Available in paperback and hardback.

To my family…for your inspiration, love, and support. Thank you.

And to pets everywhere, especially our Stu, thank you for all the love and joy you bring.

Mr. Small is a taxicab driver in New York City.

Every morning he wakes up excited to go to work.

He puts on the same blue pants, the same blue shirt, and the same brown cap.

He leaves so early in
the morning it is still
dark outside.

Mr. Small drives his yellow checker cab across town into the busy city center, passing giraffes and pigs heading to office buildings, puppies and kittens walking to school, and even elephants and rabbits hailing cabs!

Today it is rainy,
and Mr. Small has
many passengers.

On rainy days,
he doesn't see
puppies and kittens
playing in the park.

The slides are
empty, the swings
don't swing,
and the merry-go-
round doesn't look
so merry!

The rain keeps all
the animals away,
and the city doesn't
have its usual
sparkle.

Driving up and
down 5th Avenue,
Mr. Small stops
his cab, picks up
passengers and then
whisks them away.

When they arrive at
their destinations,
they are often
in a hurry and
leave some things
behind.

On rainy days, Mr. Small collects more lost items than on any other day.

Do you know what he collects?

You got it—umbrellas!

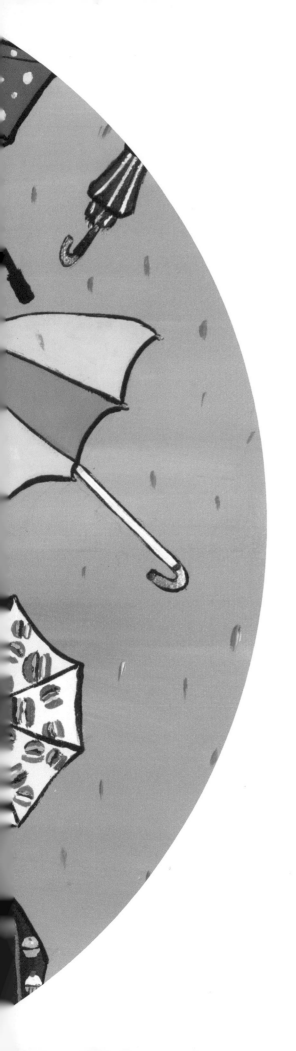

Lots and lots of umbrellas.

Pink umbrellas and
blue umbrellas, polka-dot
umbrellas and striped
umbrellas, zebra umbrellas
and cupcake umbrellas,
hamburger umbrellas,
flower umbrellas, and even
umbrellas with umbrellas
on them!

Just about any umbrella
you could ever imagine
ends up in Mr. Small's
taxicab.

At the end of each day,
Mr. Small drives home to
his wife, Mrs. Small.

When he pulls up to his
house and opens the trunk
of the cab, there are so many
lost umbrellas that they spill
out, practically toppling
Mr. Small!

He carefully gathers them
up and takes them inside his
house to Mrs. Small.

"More umbrellas?" she asks in an exasperated voice.

The Smalls have piles of lost umbrellas all over their house, umbrellas in every corner and on every chair, and now there are more!

"Whatever will we do with all these umbrellas?"

Mrs. Small is a chic cat, and she happens to be quite skilled with a sewing machine.

She sews all the curtains in their house, and sometimes she even sews Mr. Small's red socks!

On this night, after a long day of driving his taxicab in the rain, Mr. Small has a big idea.

He tells Mrs. Small all about it, and quickly, they get to work.

One by one,
Mr. Small
takes apart the
umbrellas and
cuts them up.

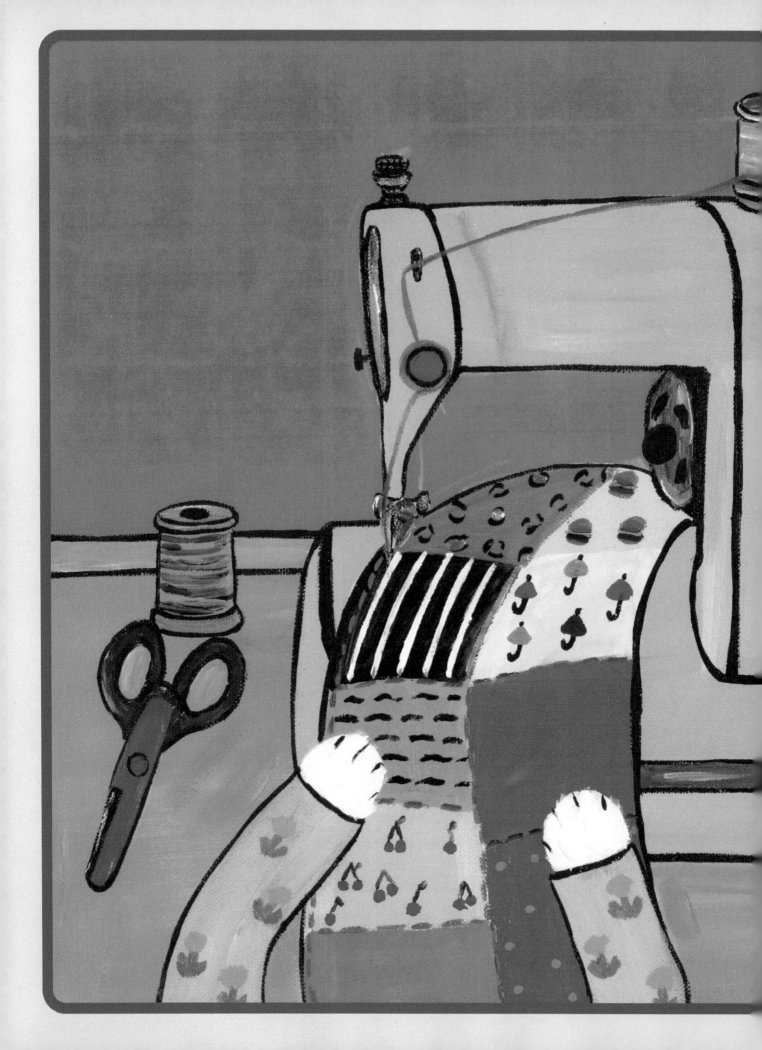

Mrs. Small busily
works at her
machine.

Cutting, sewing,
cutting, sewing.

The Smalls work all
night long, and outside
it continues to rain.

The rain goes tap, tap,
tap on the windows,

and Mrs. Small's foot goes tap, tap, tap on the sewing machine pedal.

Before they know it, it's time for Mr. Small to drive back into the city.

The Smalls carefully pack up their special project.

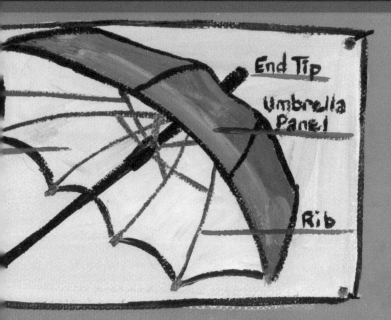

It's so big it barely fits inside Mr. Small's car!

He also packs some wood and some tools.

Mr. Small kisses Mrs. Small goodbye, and he thanks her for her help.

Driving down
Lexington
Avenue,
Mr. Small is
excited about
his big idea.

Soon he arrives at the playground in the park.

He gathers the wood,
his tools, and the
special project.

Minute by minute
and hour by hour,
Mr. Small hammers
nails and fastens
screws.

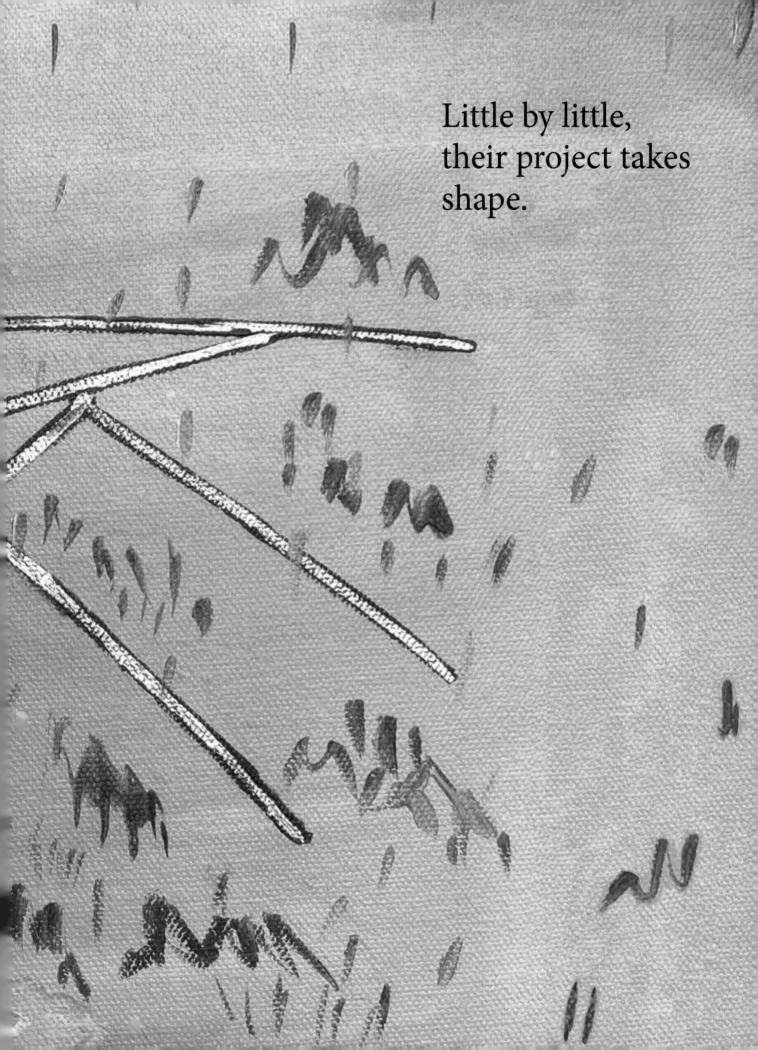

Little by little, their project takes shape.

He finishes just in time as the city begins
to wake up.

It is still raining, but he is done.

He packs up his tools and off he goes,
driving up and down the streets of
New York City.

During his lunch hour, Mr. Small drives
past the park to peek at their project.

When he turns onto
5th Avenue to make
his way to the
playground, he
can see it from a
mile away.

It is still raining, but today, animals fill the playground.

Underneath a patchwork awning of lost umbrellas, they swing, slide, and twirl—and stay completely dry the entire time.

It is a special day indeed!

Mr. Small's eyes
twinkle, and he smiles
as he drives away.

He can't wait to tell
Mrs. Small all about
their rainy-day
playground.

# EXTENSION ACTIVITIES

### •Writing:

Reflect on a rainy day that you have recently experienced. Write a short story or poem about how you like to spend rainy days and how they make you feel. Look up rainy-day poems and discuss how they differ from yours.

### •Math:

Pattern identification with the umbrellas in the book. What types of patterns do you see on the umbrellas? Make your own patterns on index cards with different types of repetition. How many different types of patterns can you come up with? Try to notice patterns in your everyday world. Where do you see them? Point them out to others when you find them.

## •Art:

Create a "Rainy-Day Playground" of your own. Make a diorama, drawing, or painting. What would your playground look like? What would you do there?

## •Cognition:

There are hidden Dalmatian mice throughout the book. How many can you spot? Want to try something a bit more challenging? How many umbrellas can you count in this book? Can you count 10 umbrellas, 20 umbrellas...how about 50 umbrellas?

## •Science:

Go outside and play in the rain. When you come inside, what happens to the water on your shoes? Research and discuss the water cycle. With adult supervision, boil a pot of water on the stove. Observe what happens to the water and discuss the states of water/matter.

# Meet Stu!

Mr. Small is based on my family's dog, Stuart Newman.

Stuart, or "Stu" as we affectionately call him at home, is a Coton de Tulear, a small breed dog, henceforth the name Mr. Small.

Stu is an absolute delight!

True to the breed's reputation, Stu acts "clownish" by standing on his hind legs and by dashing all over our house with what appears to be a smile on his face. He loves to play catch with his favorite toys, such as his gator, his monkey, or his blue blankie!

He can be found cuddling up next to our family on the sofa and burying himself under pillows and blankets while we watch television together. Stu also enjoys barking at all the squirrels and birds that visit our back patio. Although small, Stu is mighty!

# About the Illustrator

Carly Beck is an artist living in New York City. She worked for several fashion designers before turning to painting. Her playful, vibrant works include: pet portraits, interiors, exteriors, fabrics, and wallpapers. The acrylic based paintings are inspired by vintage textiles, past and present fashion collections, and the daydreams of domesticated creatures.

## About the Author

Meredith Newman is a children's book author. She writes books with lovable, whimsical characters that incorporate beautiful illustrations and meaningful lessons for young audiences.

Meredith graduated Phi Beta Kappa from Penn State University with a bachelor's degree in English, and she completed a Master's degree in Elementary Education from the University of Pennsylvania. She taught early elementary school before starting her own family.

Meredith married her high school sweetheart, and they have two children and a little dog named Stu, who are the inspiration for many of her stories. Meredith lives in Villanova, Pennsylvania and she spends time in her favorite places: Jupiter, FL and Stone Harbor, New Jersey. She enjoys: cooking, reading/writing poetry, dreaming up children's book ideas, and playing tennis and golf with her family.

## About the Designer

Chelsea Cardinal is an artist working across various mediums of design, illustration and fashion. She grew up on the Canadian prairies and now lives in Brooklyn, NY with a very silly and fluffy cat named Little Baby.

CPSIA information can be obtained
at www.ICGtesting.com
Printed in the USA
BVHW011922230323
661019BV00001B/1

* 9 7 8 1 6 3 6 8 0 1 0 7 0 *